·LAURA·RANKIN·

Fluffy and Baron

 Dial Books for Young Readers

DIAL BOOKS FOR YOUNG READERS

A division of Penguin Young Readers Group • Published by The Penguin Group
Penguin Group (USA) Inc., 375 Hudson Street, New York, NY 10014, U.S.A.

Penguin Group (Canada), 90 Eglinton Avenue East, Suite 700, Toronto, Ontario, Canada M4P 2Y3 (a division of Pearson
Penguin Canada Inc.) • Penguin Books Ltd, 80 Strand, London WC2R 0RL, England • Penguin Ireland, 25 St. Stephen's
Green, Dublin 2, Ireland (a division of Penguin Books Ltd) • Penguin Group (Australia), 250 Camberwell Road, Camberwell,
Victoria 3124, Australia (a division of Pearson Australia Group Pty Ltd) • Penguin Books India Pvt Ltd, 11 Community
Centre, Panchsheel Park, New Delhi - 110 017, India • Penguin Group (NZ), Cnr Airborne and Rosedale Roads, Albany,
Auckland 1310, New Zealand (a division of Pearson New Zealand Ltd) • Penguin Books (South Africa) (Pty) Ltd, 24 Sturdee
Avenue, Rosebank, Johannesburg 2196, South Africa • Penguin Books Ltd, Registered Offices: 80 Strand,
London WC2R 0RL, England

Text set in Bitstream Carmina • Manufactured in China on acid-free paper
1 3 5 7 9 10 8 6 4 2
Library of Congress Cataloging-in-Publication Data
Rankin, Laura.
Fluffy and Baron / Laura Rankin.
p. cm.
Summary: Chronicles the friendship between a duck, Fluffy, and a dog, Baron, from their
first meeting when Fluffy is just a duckling through the time when she has babies of her own.
Special Markets ISBN 978-0-8037-3238-4 Not for Resale
[1. Dogs—Fiction. 2. Ducks—Fiction. 3. Animals—Infancy—Fiction. 4. Friendship—Fiction.] I. Title.
PZ7+ [E]—dc22 2005003603

The art was prepared with acrylics and ink on Arches watercolor paper.

This Imagination Library edition is published by Penguin Group (USA), a Pearson
company, exclusively for Dolly Parton's Imagination Library, a not-for-profit
program designed to inspire a love of reading and learning, sponsored in part by The
Dollywood Foundation. Penguin's trade editions of this work are available wherever
books are sold.

For Mom and Dad, with love

One summer day, someone new waddled into Baron's life. Her name was Fluffy.

Baron had to share his food with her . . .

and his water.

At night, she even followed him to his favorite sleeping place.

They became friends.

Every day, the two of them played together.
Baron was good at tag.
Fluffy was great at hide-and-seek.

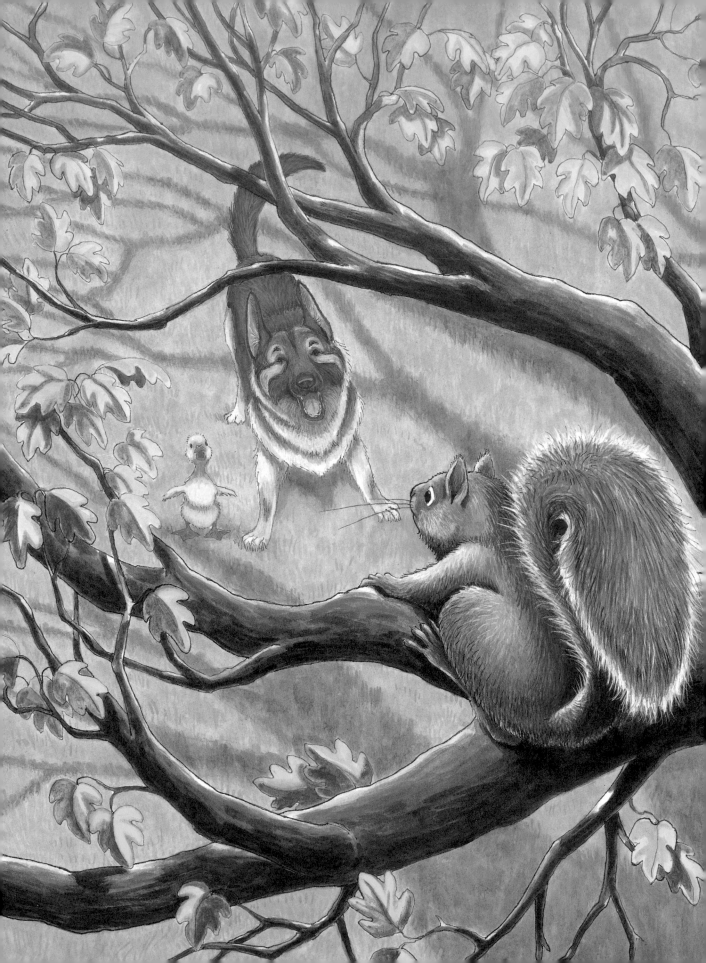

Both of them were terrific at squirrel-chasing
and fly-snapping.

As the summer passed, Fluffy grew bigger and bigger.

By autumn, she was a full-grown duck.

She and Baron stayed close and warm together all winter long.

Then spring arrived, and three wild ducks landed in the pond.
Fluffy watched, waddling back and forth—toward the newcomers
and then back to Baron again.

But finally she couldn't resist joining the other ducks. Suddenly Baron had no one to play with him.

When it was time for dinner, Fluffy still hadn't returned.
Baron had to eat alone.

For the next three nights, Fluffy didn't curl up with Baron in their favorite sleeping place.

Then the wild ducks flew away.

Baron tried to play with Fluffy, but she was too busy making a nest. She laid nine eggs in it, then gently settled herself on top and waited for them to hatch.

Four weeks later, there were ducklings!

Fluffy wanted Baron to
be the first one to meet them.
Baron's tail wagged and wagged.
Fluffy's wagged a lot too.

At last it was time to play again. And oh, what fun they all had!

That evening Baron led the way to dinner.

Never had he shared a happier meal.

And after such a busy day, everyone was eager to snuggle in together and fall asleep. Baron felt cozy and warm in his

favorite sleeping place, with nine brand-new friends and
best of all, his old friend Fluffy.

Author's Note

Fluffy and Baron *is based on many happy memories of my childhood pets, who really were best friends. Baron was a long-haired German shepherd and Fluffy was a Pekin duck.*

Pekins are a breed of domestic duck related to the Mallard. In the story, Mallard ducks are the wild ducks who visit the pond. Mallards can be found throughout the world, and although wild, are very adaptable. Some even raise their young in human habitats like city ponds, lakes, and reservoirs.

Mallards mate in the spring. A Mallard hen (female) can lay eggs for about eleven to seventeen days after mating with a male. She finds a sheltered spot near a pond, lake, or other wetland area, and makes a nest of grasses lined with her soft, downy feathers. Then the hen lays one egg each day until there are between seven and twelve eggs. She sits on—incubates—the eggs, leaving the nest only briefly for food and water, until the ducklings hatch twenty-eight to thirty days later. The drake (male duck) only stays with the hen through about the first week of incubation; male Mallards do not help to raise their young.

Soon after the ducklings hatch, usually between late April and late May, their mother teaches them how to swim, forage for food, and hide from predators. Ducklings grow rapidly; within two months their newborn down has been replaced by adult feathers and they are ready to fly.

Mallards are migratory birds. In late September and October the fall migration begins. The ducks fly from their northern breeding grounds to spend the winter in warmer wetland and coastal areas where food supplies are more plentiful. Many birds fly almost without a break. Others (such as Fluffy's visitors in this story) stop to rest and eat during the long journey. Then in February and March, the spring migration begins and the Mallards head north, once again returning to their breeding grounds.

There are many differences between wild ducks and domestic ducks like Fluffy. Mallard ducks and other wild species have lean bodies, strong, long feathers, and powerful muscles built for flight. They are born with all the natural instincts needed for survival in nature. Domestic ducks are bred to have heavy bodies and are often not capable of flight. Domestic ducks, like all pets, have been bred to rely on humans for their care, food, and shelter. It is extremely difficult for them to survive in the wild.